THIS BOOK
BELONGS TO:

....

....

Cover illustrated by Mingma Design

LADYBIRD BOOKS

UK | USA | Canada | Ireland | Australia
India | New Zealand | South Africa

Ladybird Books is part of the Penguin Random House group of companies
whose addresses can be found at global.penguinrandomhouse.com.

www.penguin.co.uk   www.puffin.co.uk   www.ladybird.co.uk

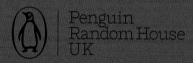
Penguin
Random House
UK

This treasury edition first published 2016
"No Room for Panda" first published in *Ladybird Stories for 3 Year Olds*, 2008
"Ernest Takes a Ride" first published in *Ladybird Stories for 4 Year Olds*, 2008

001

Printed in China

A CIP catalogue record for this book is available from the British Library

ISBN: 978–0–241–24242–1

All correspondence to:
Ladybird Books
Penguin Random House Children's
80 Strand, London WC2R 0RL

Ladybird

FIVE MINUTE STORIES

CONTENTS

NO ROOM FOR PANDA

Written by **JOAN STIMSON**
Illustrated by **INGELA PETERSON**

LUCY'S DAD WAS a sailor. He sailed the world in a big ship. When he came home, he liked to bring presents for Lucy. He got things from all the countries he visited. When he went to France, he brought Lucy back some smelly cheese. When he went to Japan, he got her some chopsticks. And when he sailed to India, he brought back a toy elephant.

One day, Lucy's dad sailed to China. When he came home, he brought a very special present. In fact you could say it was a GIANT present. Lucy's dad had brought home a panda.

Lucy was thrilled. Her mum was shocked. She didn't know if they had room for a panda. She didn't know what Panda ate or where he would sleep.

"He will eat what I eat," said Lucy. "Surely everyone likes toast and jam for tea."

That night, Panda slept in Lucy's bed. It was a bit of a squash. Still, Lucy had never had a pet before. Even though he was very big, Panda was much better than a teddy.

Lucy sighed happily and went to sleep dreaming of all the things she could do now she had a pet panda.

The next day, Lucy got ready for nursery. Then she waited at the bus stop with Mum and Panda.

"You're going to love nursery, Panda," said Lucy. "There are games to play and lots of friends to have fun with."

Panda was excited to go to nursery.

When the bus came, Panda stuck his paw out. But the bus driver was firm.

"Sorry," he said. "This panda's too big for my bus."

"Please, Mr Bus Driver? Panda has been looking forward to nursery and we don't want to be late," said Lucy.

The bus driver shook his head and drove away.

In the end, Mum, Lucy and Panda walked all the way
to nursery.

The children at Lucy's nursery were very surprised to find
a panda in the playground.

"Panda, remember your manners," said Lucy.

Panda shook hands with the boys and girls.

"What a polite panda," said Miss Roberts, the teacher.
"You are very welcome. Lucy will show you around."

Panda was keen to play with everyone.

But straight away he got stuck —
halfway down the slide!

Miss Roberts called the fire brigade.
Then she called Lucy's mum.

"I'm sorry," she said. "Panda's
too wide for nursery."

Lucy trudged home with Mum and Panda. They told Dad all about how Panda wasn't allowed on the bus and then got stuck on the nursery slide.

Lucy was sad. "It's not fair. Some things just aren't built for pandas, and he's being left out," she said.

Panda felt shy. He didn't want to get in the way.

The next day, Mum decided to take Lucy and Panda along while she did some shopping.

   Panda had never been to a supermarket. He wanted to ride in the trolley.

But Panda was too heavy. He squashed the trolley flat.

"I'm sorry," said the manager. "Your panda will have to shop somewhere else."

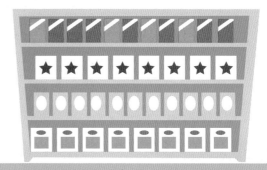

Lucy's dad felt bad. Perhaps a panda was too big a present. He wondered where Panda might fit. Then, he had a brainwave. "Let's go swimming," he said. "There will be plenty of room for Panda."

The swimming pool was perfect. There were no doors or seats or places where Panda could get stuck. To everyone's delight, Panda found that he could swim like a fish. He gave the children rides on his back. Lucy had never had so much fun at the pool.

Then Panda got too bouncy. He made great waves in the water and splashed the attendant.

The attendant blew his whistle.

"Time's up, Panda," he said. "I'm getting soaked!"

"We were just having fun," said Lucy.

"Out!" said the attendant.

Everyone went to change. Lucy's dad helped to dry Panda.

"Sorry, Panda," he said.

Mum, Dad, Lucy and Panda started to walk home. On their way they passed the zoo. Panda tugged at Lucy's hand.

"What is it, Panda?" asked Lucy.

He pointed to the zoo entrance.

"I think he wants to see the other animals," said Mum.

"You'll definitely fit in at the zoo, Panda," said Lucy. "There are lots of animals there even bigger than you!"

They decided to go in.

When they got to the gate, the zookeeper smiled at Panda.
"No charge for pandas!" he said.

Suddenly, everyone knew what to do. Mum, Dad and Lucy agreed to leave Panda at the zoo. The keeper said they could visit whenever they wanted.

Panda looked round his new home. He liked the company. He liked the space.

Mum, Dad and Lucy waved goodbye to Panda.

Then they went home – on the bus!

COCK-A-DOODLE CROAK!

Written by **MANDY ARCHER**

Illustrated by **LOUISE FORSHAW**

IT WAS THE magical moment between night and the dawn of a new day. The farm was quiet. The fields were peaceful. Farmer Johnson dozed happily in his bed. The animals snuggled up sleepily next to each other.

Only one creature noticed the sun peeping over the farmhouse roof. Desmond the cockerel puffed out his chest. It was getting-up time!

"Wake up, lambs!" he crowed. "Wake up, pigs! Wake up, Farmer Johnson!"

"Cock-a-doodle-doo!"

Every morning, at dawn, the cockerel hopped on to the henhouse roof and began to crow. The farmer didn't need an alarm clock – he had Desmond instead!

One day, Desmond woke up with a tickly, prickly feeling in his throat.

"Cock-a-doodle . . . croak!"

Poor Desmond had lost his voice! He scraped his claws. He flapped his wings. He puffed out his chest. But nobody woke up.

27

Without an alarm call, everybody slept past breakfast.
They didn't wake up until the sun was high in the sky.
Farmer Johnson was late for milking.

The sheep missed going out to the meadow.

And only half the ploughing got done.

The next morning, poor Desmond still couldn't make a sound.
The other animals slept and slept . . . and slept.

"Please wake up, Farmer Johnson," thought Desmond.
"It's market day."
Desmond tried his best, but nobody stirred.

The next day started the same way. No alarm call from Desmond meant everyone overslept again.

When the farmer finally tugged on his wellies, it was too late to go to market.

"Oh dear," he sighed. "I'll have to go next week."

But the following morning. Desmond wasn't the only one awake.

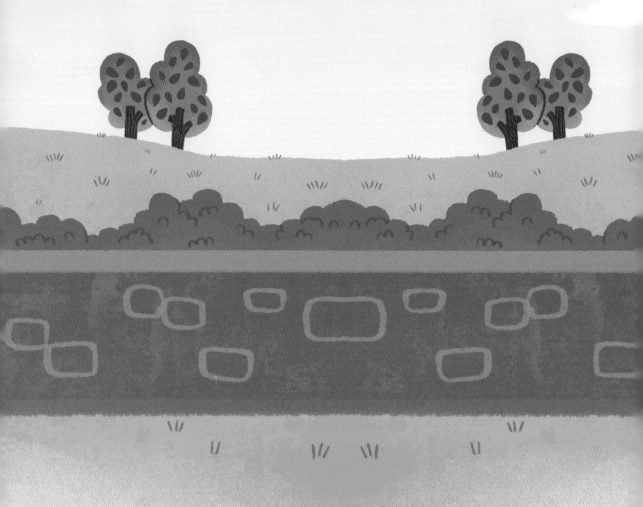

Out of the corner of his eye, he saw a bushy red tail
disappearing into the henhouse. Only one animal had
a tail like that — the fox! He was after the chickens!

This was an emergency! Desmond puffed out his chest.

"Cock-a-doodle CROAK!"

All that came out was a creaky squeak. Desmond thought fast. He strutted to the pigsty, then pecked at the water bucket.

WHOOSH! The bucket tipped over with a loud clank and a splash. The pigs oinked noisily in surprise.

Farmer Johnson heard all the
commotion and raced towards the
henhouse.

"Get out of here!" he bellowed.

The fox ran away in fright . . . without his breakfast!
Desmond had saved the chickens!

He was given a wool scarf to help his throat get better
and a horn to honk until his voice came back.

"What would we do without you?" smiled the farmer.
"You're still the very best alarm I've got."

ERNEST TAKES A RIDE

Written by **JOAN STIMSON**

Illustrated by **DEBORA VAN DE LEIJGRAFF**

ERNEST THE ELEPHANT lived in a zoo. He loved the zoo and all his friends there.

But, sometimes, Ernest wondered about life outside the zoo walls.

Ernest had a secret ambition. He wanted to ride on a red bus. There were lovely big, red buses that went past the zoo every hour, exactly on the hour.

Each day, Ernest looked out from his enclosure and saw the happy people on the bus. He wished he could join them . . . but how?

He thought long and hard about it.

"The three o'clock bus is the bus for me," thought Ernest. "Everyone will be taking a nap after lunch."

Now all he needed was the bus fare.

The next morning, Mr Wainwright the zookeeper was doing his rounds as usual.

"Good morning, Gilly Giraffe," he said as he handed out food. "Hello, Percy Panda. Hello, Lily Lion."

When Mr Wainwright reached Ernest Elephant's enclosure, he found a new notice pinned up.

Throw cash, not buns.
Am saving up.

Signed
Ernest Elephant

Mr Wainright was shocked — why would Ernest need money? Just what was that elephant up to?

The visitors loved it. In just one day, Ernest became rich.

That night, Ernest went to bed early, but he was too excited to sleep.
"Tomorrow," he kept thinking, "I shall ride on a red bus."

Eventually, he fell asleep and dreamed of
buses and all the people he would meet.

The next day, Ernest was too nervous to eat his breakfast. He was too jittery to eat his lunch.

Mr Wainwright worried that Ernest was sick. The elephant never usually left his food.

The visitors worried that Ernest was sad. He was too distracted to play with them.

Ernest couldn't concentrate. He was beginning to think that three o'clock would never come.

Ernest watched the zoo clock. At half-past two, everyone was still awake. The zoo was bustling with visitors. Maybe he would miss his chance!

At a quarter to three, there was no sign of any napping. But by five minutes to three, Mr Wainwright and the animals were all snoring soundly.

Ernest had his chance!

HEAVE! By two minutes to three Ernest had clambered on to the boundary wall of the zoo.

It was a real struggle, but Ernest just made it.

At exactly three o'clock, the red bus arrived.
Ernest had seen humans hold their arms out
to make the bus stop for them.

But Ernest couldn't get down to the pavement, and
he didn't have any arms.

Instead, he decided to dangle his trunk over the wall,
right by the bus stop.

SQUEEEEAL! The bus driver screeched to a halt. Ernest's trunk was blocking the road!

The children on board waved at Ernest. The driver was surprised to see an elephant at the bus stop. Would this elephant fit in his bus?

The bus had an open top, which lined up perfectly with the zoo wall, and Ernest stepped very gently on board. Then he settled comfortably into six seats.

The bus driver had got over his surprise, and he was beginning to feel quite important. He was looking forward to telling the other drivers he'd picked up an elephant!

But what if the elephant didn't have the bus fare?
He needn't have worried. Ernest had plenty of money.
He handed it over with a note:

Return trip to the zoo –
keep the change.
Signed
Ernest Elephant

The red bus drove through the country and into town. Ernest saw all the sights – the shops, the churches, the parks and the factories. He'd done it at last!

It was everything he had ever dreamed of. It was all so different from the zoo.

Ernest waved at the people in their houses. Some were shocked to see an elephant on a bus, but most people waved back. Ernest felt like he was a visitor at the zoo, seeing so many new things!

"I'm riding on a red bus, I'm riding on a red bus," hummed Ernest happily.

Every few minutes the bus stopped. An old lady got on with her dog. A young boy got off with his hamster.

But there were no zebras, monkeys, seals or hippos at the bus stops. There was no sight of Mr Wainwright's friendly face. Ernest began to feel homesick – homesick and hungry. It would be teatime soon and Ernest started to long for his friends.

He felt like he had been on the bus for ever. He couldn't wait for four o'clock to arrive, when the bus would be back at the stop by the zoo.

At exactly four o'clock the red bus pulled up outside the zoo.
Ernest got up from his six seats, and stepped gently back on
to the zoo wall.

   THUD! Ernest was back in his enclosure. Mr Wainwright
and the animals had stopped snoring.
They were beginning to stir.

"It's great to be home," thought Ernest, and he nuzzled his trunk into Mr Wainwright's ear. Then he gave Mr Wainwright a playful push.

Ernest was glad he had had his adventure. He would never forget riding on the red bus. But he was happy to be home in time for tea.

THE PIRATE
AND THE PRINCE

Written by **MANDY ARCHER**
Illustrated by **MARK CHAMBERS**

"LAND AHOY!" Captain Katie leaned over the side of her ship and pointed at the horizon.

The crew cheered. The *Jolly Crab* was coming into port! Katie and her crew had been away sailing the seven seas for a long time. They were looking forward to docking at the port to get some more supplies. They needed to stock up on food and water for their next adventure.

As the ship docked, the town postman struggled up the ladder with a big mail sack. He was also carrying a shiny gold postcard addressed to Captain Katie.

Katie beamed. "It's from Tom!" she cried.

Tom was her cousin. He was a prince and lived far away, in the tallest turret of the tallest castle in the land.

Even though they led very different lives, Captain Katie and Prince Tom were great friends. They wrote to each other whenever they could.

Dear Katie,
What daring adventures have you been up to this time? I am bored of my castle! I wish I could get away from it all.
Love from your cousin, Tom.

A thought popped into Katie's head. She loved being a pirate . . . most of the time. But sometimes she wished she could relax a bit more and sleep on solid ground. She scribbled a reply.

Dear Tom, she wrote.
Would you like to have a week on board my ship?
While you're away, perhaps I could put my feet up in your fancy castle? I've been sailing for too long!
Lots of love, Katie.

Tom loved Katie's idea. He had heard so much about her adventures on the high seas and it sounded like fun to spend a week on board a real pirate ship!

Before you could say "shiver me timbers", the cousins set off for their holiday swap.

"Aye, aye!" Tom called, striding up the *Jolly Crab*'s gangplank and waving to Katie's crew. "What's the adventure today?"

"The decks need swabbing," a bearded pirate replied, handing him a mop.

Mopping? That was not what Prince Tom had in mind at all! But he cleaned the deck as quickly as he could, so they would soon be ready to sail off on an amazing pirate adventure.

"I'm finished!" he called.

"Good," said the bearded pirate. "Now climb up to the crow's nest and keep a lookout."

Tom frowned. That didn't sound very adventurous! In fact, it sounded quite boring. Plus, he was a tiny bit afraid of heights . . .

Katie's holiday wasn't going any better.

As soon as she arrived at Tom's castle, she was taken away by Tom's servants and scrubbed in the bath.

When she was at sea, she never had a bath, ever! She hated it. The water was too hot and it had flowery bubbles everywhere. Katie longed for the salty seawater she was used to.

After her bath, Katie sat uncomfortably on Tom's throne wearing a big, flouncy dress. Two guards waited on her hand and foot.

"Why do I have to be so smart?" she grumbled. "I can't do anything in this dress. I'll trip over!"

At bedtime, things got worse. Katie had to sleep in a big, soft four-poster bed with fluffy covers. She felt lonely and far too hot!

"I wish I was back in my hammock," she groaned.

Life in the castle just wasn't how she had pictured it. Katie had thought that being a princess would be fun, but really, it was pretty boring. She missed the noise of the sea and her rough-tough pirate crew.

It was also bedtime on board the *Jolly Crab*. The crew were all snoring loudly, and as the ship bobbed on the sea, Tom's hammock swayed bouncily from side to side.

"When will it stop?" he wailed. "I wish I was back in my big, soft bed. It's so loud here. I can't get to sleep!"

It was a long, uncomfortable night for both of them.
In the morning, Katie and Tom had made up their minds.
They wanted to go home!

On the way back, Katie and Tom passed each other on the road.

"What are you doing here?" they both asked.

"I'm sorry!" Tom sighed. "But I miss being a prince."

Katie burst into giggles. "And I miss being a pirate!"

"I can't wait to get back to the peace and quiet of my castle," said Tom.

"And I can't wait to get back to the noisy ship," said Katie. The cousins promised to write to each other again soon.

That night, Katie climbed into her hammock with relief.
The *Jolly Crab* rocked gently from side to side.

"Goodnight, Tom," she whispered happily.

At the top of the tallest castle turret, a tiny light went out.

"Goodnight, Katie," Tom yawned. "There's no place quite like home!"

WHOSE EGG?

Written by **MANDY ROSS**

Illustrated by **LOUISE FORSHAW**

TRIXIE TRICERATOPS AND Ig Iguanadon were best friends. They both loved eating plants and playing hide and seek.

One day, they were playing quietly in the swamp when . . .

"Oh! Look!" said Trixie.

"An egg!" said Ig.

Trixie and Ig examined the egg closely. It was long and speckled. It was not in a nest. Where had it come from? Whose egg was it?

"We'd better look after it until the egg's mum comes back," said Ig.

Trixie nodded. "Or one of those big, scary meat-eating dinosaurs might gobble it up for a snack."

Trixie and Ig built a nest out of twigs and leaves. Carefully, they lifted the egg into the nest.

But the egg still seemed a bit lonely all by itself in the nest.

Trixie and Ig looked at each other.

"What should we do?" asked Ig. "Do you think it will be safe here?"

"When my mum laid an egg last summer," said Trixie, "she sat on it, to keep it warm."

"Do you mean . . . ?" frowned Ig.

"Yes! We should sit on it!" said Trixie. "Me first!" And she climbed on to the egg.

"Is it working?" she said.

"Hmm," said Ig. "I'm not sure."

The two dinosaurs took it in turns to sit on the big egg.
They waited and they waited, and they sat and they sat . . .
until at last the egg began to crack. CREAK! CRACK!

   Trixie and Ig leaned in to get a closer look.
Sharp little claws poked out of the egg. A sharp little
snout followed, full of VERY sharp tiny teeth.

   "Uh oh . . ." whispered Trixie. "I think it's a baby
Tyrannosaurus rex."

   "A Tiny T," nodded Ig. "He's tiny, but he looks fierce!"

"He might eat us up! Let's run away!" cried Trixie.

Just then, Tiny T started to cry.

"Shhh, don't cry," said Ig.

"Poor little thing," whispered Trixie. "We can't leave him all alone."

"I want my mummy," sobbed Tiny T.

"Don't be sad, Tiny T," said Ig. "We'll help you find your mummy."

Trixie and Ig set off with Tiny T.

"Where would a mummy T. rex be?" wondered Trixie.

"Don't worry, we're both brilliant at hide and seek!" said Ig to Tiny T. "We'll soon find your mummy."

Ig, Trixie and Tiny T hadn't gone far when they heard thundering footsteps.

THUD! THUD! THUD!

It was Big Mummy T. rex, the fiercest carnivore in the whole swamp.

"Mummy!" squeaked Tiny T.

"Tiny T!" roared Big Mummy. "My baby!"

Big Mummy ran towards the three dinosaurs, her jaws stretched wide.

Trixie and Ig were terrified. They looked around for somewhere to hide, but they were right by the river with nowhere to go.

"Stop, Mummy!" squealed Tiny T. "You mustn't eat my friends! Trixie and Ig looked after me when I hatched."

Big Mummy stopped. She looked confused.

"You looked after my baby? Thank you!" she roared. "Then I can't possibly eat you . . . today."

Hearts beating with relief, Ig and Trixie watched Big Mummy and Tiny T stomp away together.

"What nice friends you have, Tiny T," said Big Mummy, looking wistfully over her shoulder. "They do look tasty."

From then on, Big Mummy and Tiny T – who wasn't quite as tiny as he had been – always waved when they saw Trixie and Ig playing in the swamp. And Trixie and Ig always waved back . . . from a safe distance.

THE BACK-TO-FRONT BAT

Written by **MANDY ARCHER**
Illustrated by **MARK CHAMBERS**

RODNEY THE BAT opened his eyes and stretched his wings.
The birds were singing and the sun was shining.
Morning had arrived.

"Oh no!" he gulped. Bats were meant to sleep all day
and stay up all night. Rodney had overslept!

Rodney looked around. His friends were all asleep.

"Is anyone awake?" he called out, hopefully.

"Shh!" squeaked a voice. "It's bedtime!"

But Rodney couldn't get back to sleep. He'd been asleep for hours already!

Rodney looked over at the cave entrance. Light was pouring in. It was warm on his face. It felt nice. Maybe the daytime wasn't so scary after all . . .

Rodney's back-to-front day began. He ventured out of the cave and looked around in the bright daylight.

"Where shall I go for breakfast?" he wondered.

Bats liked to eat bugs and berries, but Rodney couldn't see any nearby. His stomach grumbled loudly.

"Who's there?" called a squirrel in the big oak tree.

"I'm Rodney," said the bat. "I'm lost and hungry."

"Eat with us!" said another squirrel. Five squirrels scampered down the tree trunk and shared out a big pile of acorns.

Rodney joined them and nibbled nervously on a nut. It didn't taste delicious – it was too hard. He decided to move on.

"Thank you for the nuts," he said, politely. The squirrels waved him goodbye.

The sun rose higher. Rodney felt hot and bothered. He flapped his wings harder, trying to create a cooling breeze.

"Who's there?" croaked a frog.

"I'm Rodney," said the bat. "I'm lost and I'm too hot."

"Sit with me on this lily pad!" said the frog. "It's cool and shady down here."

"What a friendly frog," thought Rodney. Perhaps the pond wasn't too bad after all.

Rodney swooped down to the water, but landed awkwardly, with a splash! The frog thought that was a great game and jumped into the water, splashing Rodney back.

"Ugh!" spluttered Rodney. "This is no place for a bat."
Rodney didn't like the hot sun and the splashy water. He missed
the moonlight and the cool, dark shadows of night-time.

"I feel lonely out here on my own," he sighed.

"Come and see us!" chirped the birds. "We'll sing to you!"

Rodney landed on a branch and got comfy.

"How odd!" the birds screeched. "You're upside down!"

Rodney sighed. All bats rested that way.

"You're funny-looking," said one of the birds. "Where are your feathers?"

"I don't have feathers," said Rodney. "I'm a bat."

"But how do you fly if you don't have feathers?" asked another bird.

Rodney was cross. He didn't like all the birds' questions.

"That's it," he decided. "I'm off."

The back-to-front bat slowly flapped his way back home.

   On his way, he saw Carla the cat lazing on a nearby porch.
Carla came out at night, too.

   "What are you doing up, Carla?" asked Rodney. "Aren't you tired?"

   "I never get tired," she purred. "I know how to catnap!
Instead of one big sleep, I take lots of little ones instead.
That's how I stay awake so late."

   Rodney yawned. Maybe he needed a catnap, too.

Back in the cave, Rodney found his favourite spot and fell asleep. That evening, as soon as the moon appeared, Carla came by and miaowed loudly to wake him up.

"Thank you, Carla," Rodney said.

Carla's eyes flashed. "You've had your first 'batnap'!" she said.

Rodney couldn't wait to fly out and enjoy the night. The other bats started to stretch and wake up, too.

"My batnap was good," Rodney decided. "But from now on I'm going to do things the right way round!"

A TALE
FOR TEDDY

Written by **MANDY ARCHER**
Illustrated by **MARK CHAMBERS**

IT WAS DARK outside. The moon was shining. The stars were twinkling.

Freddie rubbed his eyes and yawned.

"Time for bed, young man," said Mum, switching on the night light.

"I'm ready for bed," said Freddie, "but Waffle is not!"

Waffle was Freddie's teddy bear. He loved him very much. Freddie never went to bed without Waffle!

"I don't know where Waffle is," said Freddie.

Mum and Dad and Freddie looked around for Waffle. Where could he be?

Mum looked in Freddie's toy chest. She found some socks and a book, but no Waffle.

Dad looked on the bookshelf and in Freddie's cupboards. He found a rocket and a chocolate bar, but no Waffle. Freddie looked under his bed. He found a yo-yo and some more socks, but no Waffle.

Then Freddie had an idea. He ran out of his bedroom and along the landing.

He tugged on the bathroom light. "Here he is!"

Mum and Dad peeked into the bathroom. There was Waffle, sitting on the basin.

"I thought I'd lost you, Waffle! Are you OK? Were you hiding?" asked Freddie. He gave his teddy bear a big hug.

"Come on, Freddie," said Dad.

"But Waffle needs his nose washed and his fur brushed!" said Freddie.

Mum sighed. She fetched the brush. Dad frowned.
He fetched the sponge. Freddie carefully washed the teddy's
nose and brushed his fur. He made sure that Waffle was as clean
and fresh as he could be. Then he dried him with a big, soft towel.

   "There you go," said Mum. "Waffle's now clean, fluffy and
ready for bed."

   Freddie shook his head.

"Waffle's thirsty," said Freddie. "Can we get him a drink?"

"All right," agreed Mum. "Just a little one."

Mum fetched two glasses of milk.

"Thanks!" grinned Freddie. "That's his favourite."

When Freddie had finished his milk, he helped Waffle drink his, too.

Freddie then told Waffle all about his day — the best bits AND the worst bits. Waffle could have listened for hours, but Dad sent them up to bed.

"Come on, sleepyheads, lights out, please," said Dad.
Freddie shook his head.

"Waffle's just not feeling sleepy," shrugged Freddie.

Dad scratched his head. Waffle and Freddie really were having trouble getting to sleep tonight.

"OK," said Dad, "first let's get Waffle comfy."

Freddie and Waffle climbed into bed and Dad tucked them both in.

"Do you feel sleepy now?" asked Dad.

"It's not me, it's Waffle who isn't sleepy," said Freddie.

"Why don't you both try counting sheep?" asked Dad.

Freddie shook his head. "Waffle doesn't see the point in counting sheep, Dad. What are the sheep doing?"

Dad called Mum in.

"Is Waffle still awake?" asked Mum.

Freddie nodded his head.

"Well," said Mum, "let's fluff up his pillows."

Freddie and his teddy leaned forward so that Mum could get their pillows just right. Freddie snuggled up next to Waffle. The bed felt cosy.

But Waffle still wasn't sleepy!

"It's really time to go to sleep now. Just try closing your eyes," said Dad.

Freddie closed his eyes. Then he opened them again. "Please can Waffle have a story?" he asked.

Mum and Dad looked at each other and smiled. They sat down on the edge of Freddie's bed.

"Once upon a time," whispered Dad, "there was a little boy called Freddie . . . and a brave teddy bear called Waffle." Mum, Dad and Freddie took turns to tell the story.

Freddie and Waffle . . .

. . . sailed the seven seas,

. . . dined with a dragon,

chased after monsters . . .

. . . then made music on the moon.
It was the most amazing teddy tale ever!

Freddie snuggled a little deeper under the covers.

"Waffle likes this story," he yawned. "What happens next?"

Dad gently turned down the light.

"They lived happily ever after," he said. "Night, night."

Nobody answered. Freddie and his teddy were already fast asleep!